For Rafael

Are We There, Yeti?

Requests for permission to make copies of any part of the work should be submitted online at info@mascotbooks.com or mailed to Mascot Books, 560 Herndon Parkway #120, Herndon, VA 20170.

PRT0415A
Printed in the United States
ISBN-13: 978-1-62086-974-1
Library of Congress Control Number: 2015902751
www.mascotbooks.com

Are We There, Yeti?

Kerry Morris

Illustrated by Taylor Freshley

Hoss sat tall and alert on the hillside overlooking his village. He was a Tibetan Mastiff, a guardian of this land. He patrolled and protected it each night while the people slept. There were many hazards in the foothills of the Himalayas, but Hoss was very brave.

As he surveyed, Hoss heard a strange sound. He silently trotted toward it, crouched down, and peeked over the ledge from where the sound came. There, lying in long sheaths of grass, was a yeti.

Hoss' hackles went up and he prepared to attack. Yetis were rare and rumored to be very dangerous. The yeti was crying, though, and trembling from the cold night air. As Hoss relaxed and stood upright, the yeti saw him, curled up tighter, and hid its face in its paws.

"Please do not hurt me," it whimpered. The yeti was only a baby, and it was clearly lost and afraid.

Hoss lay down beside it and covered it with his tail. "Try to sleep until the sun rises. Then I will take you home."

"Wake up, yeti," Hoss whispered as he nudged it softly under its arm. The yeti yawned and stretched. "Now I will take you home. Where do you live?"

The baby yeti pointed to the top of the tallest mountain in the Himalayas. Hoss realized what a long, treacherous journey it would be. He had promised to take the yeti home, though, so they set off.

Outside the village, Hoss and the yeti entered a forest. A lovely song lilted from the trees. The higher they went, the louder it grew until they spotted a glossy red bird land on a branch. All of a sudden, the bird began to beat its long wings so hard it shook the branches mightily. A cloud of bright insects burst from the tree in a frenzy, and the fiery bird gobbled as many as it could.

The bird returned, humming its happy tune to say hello. "I'm a scarlet minivet, but some call me a bird of paradise because of my sweet song." She edged closer to the trunk and dropped bugs into a nest of grass and twigs. The nest gleamed in the sunrays sneaking through the leaves. "It's bound together with spiders' webs to keep it strong when I shake the tree." A tiny bird peeked over the edge.

They left the scarlet minivets to their breakfast. *"Are we there, yeti?"* Hoss asked.

"No, not yet."

As they climbed higher, something hurtled across their path. Hoss crouched low to protect the yeti. A face appeared through the brush. Soon more faces peered out. Finally, an old, dignified monkey stepped out. "We are the gray langurs," he announced. "We are having a picnic. Please come!"

They came to a lush meadow filled with monkeys. As the baby yeti sat down to eat, the monkey elder began a story. "Long ago, someone named Hanuman started a massive fire while rescuing a princess. See our black faces and hands? They were made this way by the ash. It is why people call us Hanuman langurs."

After the picnic, they began a parade of all the noises they could make. They demonstrated whoops, coughs, barks, screams, pants, grunts, honks, rumbles, and hiccups. The yeti gasped and laughed at the pageant of sounds.

At the end, Hoss barked, panted, and then rumbled, *"Are we there, yeti?"*

"Not yet," the baby yeti giggled.

The mountain was becoming
steeper. The yeti grew tired
and began to lag behind. "Keep
up, yeti," encouraged Hoss. "It is
dangerous in this area."

The baby yeti yelped in pain, and Hoss spun
around just in time to see a snake bite its little
arm. Hoss lunged forward and grabbed the snake,
shook it hard, and then flung it over the edge of the
mountain. The yeti held out its arm and cried, "It hurts!
Please help me!" But Hoss did not know what to do. He did
not have an antidote and the village was too far.

Hoss heard hoof-steps approaching.
Down the mountain a goat was running and
jumping with great agility. "Move aside!" he
commanded. The goat cleared his throat and
spit right onto the yeti's arm. Instantly, the
venom dissolved. "I'm a markhor goat," the healer explained.
"My name comes from the Persian words meaning snake-eater.
People believe that I eat snakes and the foam from my mouth when
I chew will extract poison from snakebites."

"Folklore or not, you have saved the baby yeti. Thank you," said Hoss humbly.

The markhor goat lifted the yeti on his back to ride behind his snake-shaped horns. *"Are we there, yeti?"* Hoss asked as he helped it up.

"Not yet."

The markhor goat dropped off the yeti on a large plateau and left to return home. "We must find a place to spend the night," Hoss cautioned. "It will get very cold now that the sun has set." They saw a column of smoke rising in the distance.

"A fire!" the yeti announced. But it was not a fire, and it was not smoke. They soon realized that it was steam, rising from the breath of many wooly cows huddled together. One of them turned and noticed the yeti shivering. It grunted a command, and the herd surrounded Hoss and the yeti.

In the warm center, the calves were getting ready for bed. "We are yaks. You can sleep here with us," one said as she brushed her long, matted hair. "We love the cold and have special features to live in it. Our lungs and hearts are larger than other cows and we have a sticky substance that insulates us!"

"You smell!" said another to the yeti.

A mother yak thumped him on the rump. "Our fur is odor-resistant," she explained. "They are not used to the scents of other animals yet."

They fell asleep with sheets of steam swirling around their wooly beds. Far away, as in a dream, the yeti heard, *"Are we there, yeti?"*

"Not yet," it snored.

With a full night's rest and a breakfast of yak's milk, Hoss and the yeti continued climbing. It was not long before Hoss realized they were lost. Trying to stay calm, he barked to call for help.

"Marco!" they heard from behind them. Hoss was confused.
"Polo!" a voice rang out from somewhere else.

Back and forth the voices shouted until the one found the other and two sheep with great, curved horns fell onto their backs laughing. "Again!" shouted the sheep.

"Excuse me," Hoss interrupted gently. "Can you help us past this rock maze?"

The sheep jumped up excitedly. "We will make a game of it! We are Marco Polo sheep, named after the explorer who discovered us. We will lead you through by sound." They scampered off, giggling and pushing. "Marco!"

The yeti climbed onto Hoss' back and cupped its paws around its mouth. "Polo!" it bellowed.

After a few minutes, they found the Marco Polo sheep laughing and kicking their feet at the edge of the rock field. Hoss breathed a sigh of relief. *"Are we there, yeti?"*

"Polo!" shouted the yeti.

Hoss and the yeti reached the timberline, the altitude where trees stop growing. Just past it, the yeti spotted something. "Daddy!" it shouted.

As they neared, a bear turned around and stood up to face them. The yeti froze and became frightened. The bear was huge and black with a tinge of blue to his fur. He seemed angry. "You are trespassing!" he boomed.

Hoss shielded the baby yeti. "This yeti is lost and I am taking it home. We did not mean to trespass. May we pass through your territory?"

"I will let you pass, but only if you can tell me more names for my species than I can. I am one of the rarest bears in the world."

As a guardian, Hoss knew much about this bear's kind. They went back and forth, listing his names: Tibetan blue bear, Tibetan brown bear, Himalayan blue bear, Himalayan snow bear, horse bear, and mountain bear.

It was Hoss' turn but he could not remember any more names. The yeti clutched Hoss' front leg in worry, and the fog of its breath rose to his snout, reminding him of the yak's column of steam. "A yak bear!" Hoss recalled.

The bear rose to his full height and roared, "Go! You may pass. This time…"

They hustled past the bear as fast as they could. *"Are we there, yeti?"* Hoss asked as he looked back at the massive silhouette on the hillside.

"Not yet."

Hoss and the baby yeti were almost at the top. They had to take more breaks because of the extreme cold and wind. Sitting against a snow bank, a gust of wind blew shimmering snow across their view. When it passed, there was a snow leopard standing in its place. Her stocky, muscular body was covered in grayish-white fur, speckled with black rosettes. She had piercing blue eyes, light and powdery like a glacier. Hoss stood defensively as the leopard approached.

"Don't fear," she purred as she flicked her tail back and forth. "I'm only curious. You have a yeti with you and I've never met one." Suddenly, the snow leopard jumped all the way over Hoss and landed on the other side of the yeti.

She sniffed and nudged it. Her tail curled around it like a boa constrictor. The yeti held its paw against hers. It was smaller, but they were both wide like natural snowshoes.

The wind blew hard again and just as quickly as she appeared, the snow leopard was gone.

Hoss checked the yeti. "Are you alright?"

"Yes, she did not hurt me."

They set off on the last leg up the mountain. *"Are we there, yeti?"*

"Not quite."

Hoss and the baby yeti stepped onto the peak of Mount Everest. They simply stood and looked out at the breathtaking view. They were more than 5 miles above sea level. It was the highest spot in the world. *"Are we there, yeti?"*

Behind them, they heard a relieved gasp. "Mom! Dad!" the baby yeti cried.

They ran into each other's arms. "We have been so worried about you!"

"I got lost," explained the baby. "Hoss found me, protected me, and brought me home."

The yeti family was so grateful. They made Hoss supper and shared stories about Mount Everest. "The Himalayas are the third largest deposit of snow and ice on earth. Only the North and South Poles have more. In fact, we have 15,000 glaciers here, the biggest being 48 miles long!"

Before he left, Hoss hugged the baby yeti hard.

"Thank you for taking me home," whispered the yeti.

"Thank you for such an adventure," replied Hoss. From that day forward, Tibetan Mastiffs and yetis were dear friends and allies.

About the Author

**Kerry rescued Hoss from a humane society after he was
found roaming in the mountains. They instantly bonded,
and Hoss has been a loyal, gentle guardian ever since.**

Have a book idea?
Contact us at:

Mascot Books
560 Herndon Parkway
Suite 120
Herndon, VA 20170

info@mascotbooks.com | www.mascotbooks.com